D0283256

NINETEEN NINETEEN

NINETEEN NINETEEN

HUGH BRODY
AND
MICHAEL IGNATIEFF

With an Afterword by John Berger

faber and faber
LONDON · BOSTON

First published in 1985
by Faber and Faber Limited
3 Queen Square London WC1N 3AU

Printed in Great Britain by
Redwood Burn Limited,
Trowbridge, Wiltshire

All rights reserved

© Hugh Brody and Michael Ignatieff, 1985
Afterword © John Berger, 1985

This book is sold subject to the condition that it shall not, by way of trade or otherwise, be lent, resold, hired out or otherwise circulated without the publisher's prior consent in any form of binding or cover other than that in which it is published and without a similar condition including this condition being imposed on the subsequent purchaser.

British Library Cataloguing in Publication Data

Brody, Hugh
Nineteen nineteen.
I. Title II. Ignatieff, Michael
823'.914[F] PR6052.R5/

ISBN 0–571–13714–8

Nineteen Nineteen is a work of fiction inspired by case histories written by Sigmund Freud. It does not purport to represent actual relationships between Freud and any of his patients.

CONTENTS

ACKNOWLEDGEMENTS

For their help in the preparation of this book we would like to thank Nita Amy, Walter Donohue, Andy Powell and Mary Jane Walsh, all of the British Film Institute. For permission to reproduce the photographs that appear in the book we acknowledge with gratitude Will Appelt of Vienna (pp. 76 77 79 80 90 91); David Bramley (pp. 38 41 46 55); Clive Coote (pp. 20 25 34 40 65 69 70 74); Stanley Foreman of Educational and Television Films Ltd (pp. 32 45 61); and Marvin Lyons (pp. 29 58).

INTRODUCTION

HUGH BRODY AND MICHAEL IGNATIEFF

The rooms are dark, their windows hung with lace curtains, the floors carpeted with worn Persian rugs. The furniture is heavy and old. Shelves packed with books and papers stretch up to the ceilings. On tables, in cabinets, even on the writing desk there are crowds of figurines – gods and goddesses of vanished cultures – and curious archaeological finds. Against the far wall of the consulting room, between a tiled stove and a Roman head on a pedestal, there is a *chaise-longue*, a worn chair and a low footstool.

In 1938, a few weeks before Freud fled the Nazis and boarded a train to London, Edmund Engelman photographed Freud's rooms in every detail. We looked at the photographs – at these crowded, silent rooms – and began to talk about a film in which Freud would be an absence rather than a presence – a voice heard over the shoulder. We were drawn to the Freud who had vanished from these photographs, the man who still escapes our certainties.

We were also drawn to Freud at the end of the First World War, in a city filled with beggars, at the centre of an empire in ruins. He was already 60 years old, his savings gone, without even the money to heat his consulting room.

At this time Freud wrote one of his least-known papers: 'The Psychogenesis of Homosexuality in a Woman' (1920). Other cases of his – Dora, Ratman, Wolfman – are dense and complex, with the manoeuvres of analyst and analysand recorded as Freud wished to remember them. But 'The Psychogenesis' is thin and incomplete; there are hints of a young woman's struggle, a challenge to Freud's authority. But we felt that the logic of the struggle, the real story, remained hidden. Here was a mystery, an incitement to fiction . . .

We gave the young woman a name: Sophie Rubin. We began to imagine her and the events that lay behind her treatment. Then we imagined her life after she walked out of the consulting room for the last time: emigration to New York, life in a new country, a marriage . . . Soon we had created a Sophie who, even on the couch, even in dialogue with Freud, had become a fiction. And, as fiction, the story began to move from the past to the present, from Sophie as a young woman to an old Sophie struggling with her memories.

In our story Sophie suddenly resolves to confront her past, in which Freud now figures as a problem among problems: she must return to Vienna. But to whom can she return? There is only one possibility: another patient. But which one?

Of the cases that Freud mentions in 1919, there was one who seized our imagination: a Russian aristocrat, a depressive who had turned up at Berggasse (we supposed) on a leisurely tour of the nerve doctors and rest cures of Europe. This was the Wolfman, the most famous of all Freud's patients, the man who dreamed a masterpiece of Freudian dreaming: seven white wolves in a tree staring through an open window at the child awake in his cot. But of the Wolfman as anything but a child, of the person himself, the case tells very little. And there was another mystery, soon confirmed, that the Wolfman had limped from treatment to treatment, befriended and supported by the American analyst Muriel Gardiner but then disappearing into obscurity upon her departure from Vienna in 1938. Here was a man whose life had been shaped by momentous events – the Bolshevik Revolution, the Nazi occupation of Austria – but whose neurosis Freud traced back, outside history, to an eternal conflict of infantile desire. Here was a patient whose whole existence seemed to have been impaled – but on what? Childhood traumas? Contact with Freud's authority? Or the largest of circumstances? We set about imagining the events that Freud's account leaves out. In this way we invented a new character. We gave him a name: Alexander Scherbatov.

We now had the person – the destination – for Sophie's return. We imagined an encounter between her and Alexander. The story began to develop a new impetus. With each line of dialogue the characters, including Freud, stepped farther and farther away from their originals. *Nineteen Nineteen* became a film set in modern Vienna. Sophie and Alexander are caught again and again by the painful momentum of memory. In Alexander's apartment, in the Prater Gardens, in modern streets, recollection emerges as obsession. As a result, some of the old questions – about the meaning of Freud, the efficacy of psychoanalysis – became less urgent. New questions took shape: How could these two people make sense of lives fractured by history? Was there some possible reconciliation for them, even between them? What is to be found at the intersection of public history and private fate?

We began with some photographs of vanished Viennese rooms, with some case histories, and we ended with a script about a man and a woman in their late sixties, in search of each other, in search of the impalpable shape of human life, one afternoon in Vienna.

When the script was turned into a film, other forces started to work their changes. Characters became actors, each of whom had his or her own understanding of their part in the story. In the course of rehearsals some scenes grew, others faded away. Then came sets, locations and even weather: Alexander's apartment was built and furnished and acquired its own life; the choice of a Viennese café created unexpected opportunities; the wettest spring in Austrian history caused exterior scenes to be rewritten on the spot. The practicalities of film-making opened a gulf between script and film.

The script printed here is a compromise between the draft on the eve of rehearsals and the film itself. We have not always edited dialogue on the page to be true to the film. Conscious of how difficult it can be to read film scripts, with their cumbersome headings and irritatingly partial visualizations, we have tried to leave dialogue that makes the stories easier to follow. It is impossible to edit a script to take account of silent scenes, the rhythm of images on a screen or the meanings that actors give to their lines. A film script is inevitably a sort of elaborate shorthand.

On the other hand, some scenes that were dropped during rehearsals have stayed out, and scenes that were added during the shooting and editing of the film have been left in. Newsreel sequences and still photographs that were not anticipated in our earlier versions, but that appear in the film, are here included. And the overall shape of the story is more faithful to the way the film was edited than to our final draft.

In the end *Nineteen Nineteen* was written to be seen. What we can hope for is that seeing and reading it will be complementary pleasures.

Nineteen Nineteen opened at the Curzon Cinema, London in spring 1985.

Cast:

ALEXANDER SCHERBATOV	Paul Scofield
SOPHIE RUBIN	Maria Schell
FREUD	Frank Finlay
ANNA	Diana Quick
YOUNG SOPHIE	Clare Higgins
YOUNG ALEXANDER	Colin Firth
NINA	Sandra Berkin
SOPHIE'S FATHER	Alan Tilvern

Crew:

Art Director	Caroline Amies
Director of Photography	Ivan Strasburg
Editor	David Gladwell
Music	Brian Gascoigne
Producer	Nita Amy
Executive Producer	Peter Sainsbury

Based on an idea by Michael Ignatieff

Director Hugh Brody

1. INT. VIENNA. DAY

A hallway of a Viennese apartment building in the 1920s. Sounds of the city; footsteps on the pavement outside. An ornate stairwell opens from the hallway. Wide stone steps climb to a heavy, dark apartment door. A brass name plate: DR SIGMUND FREUD.

We see the hall, the steps, the door as if through the eyes of someone making his or her way to FREUD*'s rooms. The sounds of the city fade into the distance, into silence.*

Inside the door: a group of statues stands on a table in the consulting room. We look across the room – bookcases, cabinets crammed with figurines, the famous couch, a stove – and, through the archway, to FREUD*'s study. We drift through rooms filled with a chaotic accumulation of artefacts, papers, books: insignia of Central European culture.*

We see objects in a cabinet, so close as to be abstractions.

2. INT. SOPHIE'S APARTMENT, NEW YORK. NIGHT

SOPHIE *on a television screen: the image is grainy, the face is fatigued. A woman in her middle sixties, handsome but worn by life.*

SOPHIE: It was a hard year for him. He was 63. He had lost his savings. Then his daughter died . . . I only learned afterwards . . . when I had been his patient, you see.

(*In* SOPHIE*'s New York apartment a wine glass is on a low table and* SOPHIE *is watching herself on the screen.*)

God, I look awful.

(ALEXANDER *appears on the screen: a craggy, troubled face, with a certain air of distraction and neglect. He is also in his middle sixties.*)

ALEXANDER: He was very thin. I used to think, *he* is the one who is sick. Three years later . . . I think . . . his cancer began. I was not surprised.

(*An awkward pause.* ALEXANDER *shifts his position uncomfortably.* SOPHIE, *watching the TV intently, edges slightly closer.*)

His voice was . . . full of . . . authority. Nothing escaped him. Nothing.

INTERVIEWER: (*An American voice; a hint of impatience with a difficult interviewee*) Were you cured?

ALEXANDER: (*Abstracted, slow, looks down at his hands folded in his lap*) I read everything of his, you know. He says somewhere . . . (searching for words) . . . what was it? 'There are no cures . . . Only the possibility of converting hysterical misery into everyday unhappiness.' Something like that.

INTERVIEWER: Was that good enough for you?

ALEXANDER: (*Edgy*) Yes . . . yes . . . What else is possible? (*As an afterthought*:) He was . . . a great man.

(*A breakfast cereal advertisement interrupts the TV programme, breaking the mood with its inconsequential chatter.* SOPHIE *continues to stare at the screen with a look of anguish on her face. A decision is forming in her mind. She lights a cigarette. The sounds of the advertisement slowly fade away, leaving* SOPHIE *in silent concentration.*)

3. EXT. VIENNA AIRPORT. AFTERNOON

Roar of airport noise. SOPHIE *appears through the automatic doors leading to the airport concourse and makes her way to a taxi.*

SOPHIE: Hotel Römische Kaiser, *bitte*.

4. EXT. MOTORWAY INTO THE CITY. AFTERNOON

SOPHIE, *sitting in the back seat of a taxi, stares out at a landscape changed beyond all recognition: signs to Bratislava, Budapest and Vienna flash by overhead. She lights a cigarette and watches the high dark apartment buildings of Vienna, the trams and the city monuments. She is lost in thought and recollections. Over her face in profile she hears, as if in a dream, her own voice as a young woman.*

YOUNG SOPHIE: (*Voice over*) I've got another dream to tell you. I was on holiday. I was walking down to the lake.

5. INT. FREUD'S ROOMS. DAY

YOUNG SOPHIE *is lying on the couch in the consulting room. The shot takes in the couch, the rug on the wall, Ingres'* Oedipus and the Sphinx *hanging over the couch.* YOUNG SOPHIE *is wrapped up in a fur coat, giving a slightly shivery appearance. It is very cold.*

FREUD *is not, and never will be, visible. But his voice is not that of a hidden god; he has a weary, avuncular tone.*

YOUNG SOPHIE: I think I wanted to swim. There was a man on one side of me and a small child on the other. No one I know. We were holding hands . . . As we came down to the lake, I noticed a head pop up above the water. He wasn't swimming: he seemed to surface, like a creature from the deep.
(YOUNG SOPHIE *smiles, then blushes slightly.*)
He had a grey beard, and was very thin . . .

6. EXT. VIENNA TAXI. AFTERNOON

SOPHIE *watches the strange cityscape passing by, but her attention is still held by the voice inside her memory.*

FREUD: (*Voice over; with quiet humour*) Were you glad to see me?

YOUNG SOPHIE: (*Voice over*) No . . . not at first. (*Emphatically*) No. I had so wanted for us – me and the man and the child – to be alone there. Then I recognized you and was delighted to see you. (*Pause.*) Do you often surface in people's dreams?

FREUD: (*Voice over*) All the time, but in my bathing costume not so often. (*Pause.*)

YOUNG SOPHIE: (*Voice over*) I dreamed myself a family!

FREUD: (*Voice over*) You dreamed yourself a cure. (*Pause.*) You know, I think your dream is lying.

7. EXT. VIENNA STREET. DUSK

The taxi draws up in front of the Hotel Römische Kaiser. SOPHIE *gets out, takes her bags, walks along the narrow entrance alley. Dark, heavily Central European façades rise above her.*

YOUNG SOPHIE: (*Voice over*) But I *did* have the dream.

FREUD: (*Voice over*) Yes. Yes. But what dream? What *wishes*? A wish to do as your father would like? That is your conscious . . .

YOUNG SOPHIE: (*Voice over*) And my unconscious?

FREUD: (*Voice over*) Perhaps you should tell me . . .

8. INT. FREUD'S ROOMS. DAY

YOUNG SOPHIE *is lying on the couch, a look of restless exasperation on her face.*

YOUNG SOPHIE: I came here in such a good mood . . .

FREUD: (*Amused*) And now you are angry. That is your unconscious. Your dream springs from there. (*Slowly*) It is the fulfilment of a wish . . .

YOUNG SOPHIE: (*Getting angrier*) But *what* wish?

FREUD: A wish to deceive.

YOUNG SOPHIE: Who?

FREUD: (*Quietly, wearily*) Me.

9. EXT. PRATER GARDENS, 1918. DAY

A flash of joyful memory: YOUNG SOPHIE *hurtles down the water chute at the funfair, screaming with delight. At the bottom, a beautiful face in profile –* ANNA'*s. She smiles knowingly but lovingly.*

10. EXT. VIENNA STREETS, 1920S. DAY

Black-and-white newsreel images: bustling streets, trams, women at a flower stall: the lost Vienna of Sophie's youth.

11. EXT. VIENNA COURTYARD. DAY

SOPHIE, *carrying a bunch of anemones, is looking for Alexander's apartment. She enters a complex of very old and run-down courtyards. She makes her way up steps and through arches: dilapidated walls and unfamiliar doorways are closing in around her. As she mounts a staircase, Russian choral music drifts from a radio or record player in an upstairs room.*

12. INT. ALEXANDER'S APARTMENT. DAY

SOPHIE *is standing in a hallway in front of a door. She rings the brass doorbell. She can hear the choral music through the door. She waits. A commotion is heard behind the door. The music stops abruptly. The door opens but catches loudly on a brass security chain. Behind the chain we see* ALEXANDER'*s face appear, wild, puzzled, distracted from private absorption. He blinks.*

SOPHIE: Alexander *Scher*batov?

ALEXANDER: (*Nods warily*) Scher*ba*tov.

SOPHIE: Sorry, Scher*ba*tov. I'm Sophie Rubin. From New York. I called from the hotel. (*Pause.* ALEXANDER'*s face remains tense, sceptical. He stares at* SOPHIE, *then shuts the door. A pause while he fiddles with the brass catch. The door opens into a dark entrance hall.* ALEXANDER *turns and walks ahead.* SOPHIE *goes in, moving uneasily past* ALEXANDER, *who makes a point of relocking and securing the door behind them.*)

ALEXANDER: (*Very awkward*) So, we were on television together, in New York. That's incredible.

(*A door at the end of the entrance hall is ajar.* ALEXANDER *pushes it open and waves* SOPHIE *in with a rather grand waiter's gesture. He is wearing a green smoking jacket, very faded but elegant.* SOPHIE *walks ahead into the main room,* ALEXANDER *following behind. She has her first glimpse of his crowded, cluttered refuge.* SOPHIE *turns around;* ALEXANDER *examines her critically.*)

ALEXANDER: You have tracked me down to my dungeon, my lair.

SOPHIE: Coming to Vienna . . . everything has changed.

ALEXANDER: Everything is the same . . . (*Agreeable, but wary*) What do you want from me?

SOPHIE: To remember.

(She looks at ALEXANDER. *She is apprehensive.* ALEXANDER *is very still, withdrawn. He stares at his room, a private museum of his past: the faded green wallpaper covered with paintings and photographs; a huge mirror on the opposite wall completely surrounded by family snapshots and postcards; a marble-topped table; an ancient* chaise-longue *in the corner, littered with papers, books, plastic shopping bags. Through long lace curtains shines the weak sunlight from the courtyard.)*

13. INT. FREUD'S APARTMENT. DAY

YOUNG ALEXANDER *lies on the couch. Muffled up in a huge*

overcoat, he is staring at the ceiling.

YOUNG ALEXANDER: I remember . . . this joke. Two little boys are playing in the mud. A man comes by and asks them 'What are you making?' 'A church.' 'Where is the priest then?' One of the little boys says, 'We haven't enough shit for a priest.'

(*The sound of* FREUD*'s laughter.*)

14. INT. CHILD'S NURSERY. PRE-REVOLUTIONARY RUSSIA. NIGHT

A dark, wood-panelled room. YOUNG ALEXANDER, *a child of 7, is in bed, listening to a Pushkin fairy story read in Russian by his nurse.*

15. INT. ALEXANDER'S APARTMENT. DAY

ALEXANDER *is standing in front of his huge mirror, lost in his photographs.*

SOPHIE: (*Gently*) Mr Scherbatov?

ALEXANDER: Where was I? Oh yes. I was showing you ... Nanya, my nurse ... That one was taken at Gaspra on the Crimea ... Mitro, the chauffeur ... My monkey ... My pony, brought all the way from England ... My sister ...

(*He picks up a picture on the dresser. It is a photograph of a small boy in a sailor suit seated at the feet of a woman in a long gown reclining on a* chaise-longue *in an ivied garden.*)

Look here. I was 7. That's my mother, recovering from one of her illnesses. Once I came to her in the garden. She was asleep. I touched her face and said, 'Mamma'. She woke with a start. Staring at me. In terror. She didn't know who I was ...

(*He pauses. He is looking at the photograph of his sister and himself. Then he points to a photograph of an aristocrat in riding breeches and a Norfolk jacket with a gun over his shoulder and three hunting dogs on a leash.*)

My father. His hunting dogs. Borzois. Bigger than I was. He would hold all three by their collars. They would be straining, champing ... like horses. He would call me over to pet them. 'They won't hurt you. They won't hurt you.' Then he would let them go. They leapt all over me. I was terrified. He laughed. 'They won't hurt you, my little fool. *Durachock, durachock.*'

16. EXT. RUSSIAN ESTATE. DAY

Two men in fencing regalia exchange lunges in a bright, leafy alley. One of them is the YOUNG ALEXANDER, *the other one his* FENCING MASTER. ALEXANDER'S SISTER *appears through an archway, leading a trio of Borzois. She laughs at her brother.* ALEXANDER *rips off his mask; his face is dripping with sweat and contorted with fury.*

17. INT. FREUD'S ROOMS. DAY

YOUNG ALEXANDER *wrapped in his greatcoat, white-faced and anxious.*

YOUNG ALEXANDER: I've been thinking about my sister. (*Hesitantly*) I remember something. That summer at the estate on the Crimea . . . I was 4, she was 7 . . . In the afternoons, when my parents were taking their nap in their rooms, we used to steal out of the nursery and . . . play together in the fields behind the lake. No one could see us. We rolled down the hill together . . . over and over. Once, I remember, I went off by myself, well, in the bushes where I couldn't see her and I was – (*He pauses, hesitates.*)

FREUD: Having a bowel movement?

YOUNG ALEXANDER: Yes. Suddenly my sister comes up behind me and starts pointing and shrieking with laughter. Shrieking. (*Drifting*) Brothers and sisters play together . . . You say it is where it all started. (*Intensely*) But why should it have such an effect on me?

18. INT. ALEXANDER'S APARTMENT. DAY

ALEXANDER *is standing by the mirror, staring at his own reflection.* SOPHIE *is watching him.*

ALEXANDER: (*Bitterly*) He thought my problem was in my mind, in my childhood. You read what he said about me? That when I first came to him I couldn't even dress without the help of a servant? That I couldn't put on my own trousers?

(*He turns from his reflection and walks away from* SOPHIE, *who watches him quizzically.*)

A complete fabrication. He just wanted to believe that I owed everything to him. (*Begins to mutter to himself*:) A mistake . . . A mistake . . .

SOPHIE: But on the television you said . . .

ALEXANDER: (*Mockingly*) The television . . . So what about the television?

(SOPHIE *moves towards* ALEXANDER. *She is still holding the flowers. She is thinking: he is very strange, this is going to be difficult . . .*)

SOPHIE: But there *was* your neurosis . . . the headaches . . .

ALEXANDER: (*Throws his hands up, ready to gesticulate, to perform*) In my family they were all crazy. My father's brother, Alyosha, had a huge estate in Orel Gubernia, thousands of *dessiatin*. He used to talk politics to his race horses, leaning on the stable door with all the stable boys listening. He swore that his best stallion, Narishkin, was a Constitutional Democrat. Alyosha,

naturally, was a Monarchist. So they were always disagreeing, he and the horses. All crazy.
(SOPHIE *chuckles and hands him the flowers.*)

19. EXT. RUSSIAN ESTATE. DAY

Black-and-white images of pre-revolutionary Russia: a corpulent aristocratic couple descend the stairs of their villa; the cupola of a village church; an expanse of fields; birch trees swaying in the wind; peasants threshing corn; peasant women

sweeping up the grain; a gleaner bent double in a field.

ALEXANDER: (*Voice over*) My father had 80,000 *dessiatin*: estates in Kherson, Orel . . . So many houses that I never even saw all of them . . . Vaska . . . Pyotr . . .

Vassili . . . little Sonia . . . Gregori Arkadovich . . . *gribi . . . gribi . . .*

20. INT. ALEXANDER'S APARTMENT. DAY

SOPHIE: What?

ALEXANDER: (*Louder, coming out of his memory to explain*) Mushrooms. Gregori Arkadovich had such a nose for mushrooms . . .

SOPHIE: They were the most exploited people on earth!

ALEXANDER: They were our . . . our . . . We picked mushrooms together. (*Almost frantic:* SOPHIE *has begun to get to him.*) I remember . . .

21. EXT. RUSSIA. DAY

Black-and-white stills of Russian faces: peasants and workers in individual close-ups; men with eyes haunted by oppression and the possibility of revolution. Then a panorama of faces in a revolutionary crowd.

22. INT. ALEXANDER'S APARTMENT. DAY

ALEXANDER *is seated on his corner couch, perplexed and at bay.* SOPHIE *is sitting forward in an armchair beside an old wood-burning stove.*

ALEXANDER: Your Americans. They are all so young. I was born before their fathers. They know nothing. They all want me to perform. It's my circus act, my memory. (*Mimicking himself*) Over here stood the cabinet of Egyptian antiquities . . . Yes, you could see *Oedipus and the Sphinx* when you looked up from the couch. The brass door handle in the corner would turn, and in he would come . . .

(*He throws down his hands, and turns away from* SOPHIE *in disgust.*)

Agh . . . I'm tired of it. I'm a relic. They all come to look at me! What's the point of it? (*Tired, rather than*

bitter) What was ever the point? (*He turns and stares at* SOPHIE.) And now you.

SOPHIE: I'm different from the others. I was *there*. You're the only one left I can talk to.

23. INT. FREUD'S ROOM. DAY

The stairs to FREUD*'s consulting room, then, through the door, Egyptian antiquities hanging on the walls, cushions on the couch, the Persian carpet on the floor – all seen from the patient's point of view.*

SOPHIE: (*Voice over*) Don't you remember how cold it was that winter? He didn't even have enough money to heat the consulting room. I lay there on the couch in my overcoat, shivering. He sat behind me, not saying much but occasionally (*Chuckles softly*) blowing on his hands to keep warm . . . (*Pause.*) He was so thin . . . wasted almost . . .

24. INT. ALEXANDER'S APARTMENT. DAY

ALEXANDER *is still on his* chaise-longue, SOPHIE *in the armchair at the other side of the room.*

SOPHIE: Did you wear your overcoat too?

ALEXANDER: I don't remember anything. Remembering . . . What's to be gained from remembering?

SOPHIE: You *do* remember . . .

ALEXANDER: Only the things I never told him. (*Softly*) He took everything else.

SOPHIE: Try.

25. INT. VIENNESE RESTAURANT. DAY

YOUNG ALEXANDER *in a waiter's tail-coat hands a tray of dishes through a hatch that leads to the restaurant kitchens. A red-faced woman, beaded with sweat, takes the dishes and leers at him. As* YOUNG ALEXANDER *walks away, she shrugs her shoulders disdainfully.*

FREUD: (*Voice over*) Say everything that comes into your mind, no matter how trivial it may seem, no matter how disturbing, or disgusting . . . (*Trails off.*)

26. INT. FREUD'S ROOM. DAY

YOUNG ALEXANDER *leaps up from the couch, staring, horrified.*

YOUNG ALEXANDER: No! No! No!

27. INT. ALEXANDER'S APARTMENT. DAY

ALEXANDER *leaps up from his* chaise-longue.

ALEXANDER: No! No! No!

(*He composes himself, then becomes very mannered.*)
Ah . . . the flowers . . .
(*He goes to the table where the bunch of anemones lies wrapped in paper. He picks it up and disappears into the kitchen. Sound of water.* SOPHIE, *still sitting in the armchair by the stove and smoking, watches* ALEXANDER *leave the room and stares for a moment at the doorway; she is realizing how difficult and unnerving this return to Vienna is proving. She is also angry: her approaches have been rebuffed. She stubs out a cigarette, gets up and walks across to the window in the farthest corner of the apartment. She picks up a large old photograph and looks at it.* ALEXANDER *returns from the kitchen, carrying the flowers stuffed in a vase. He sets them down on the table and turns to look at* SOPHIE.)

ALEXANDER: You don't look Jewish. I mean . . .

SOPHIE: (*Sardonically*) Don't I? Neither do you.

ALEXANDER: (*As if to say Judaism* is *an issue*) Oh, I'm not . . .
(*An awkward pause.*)

SOPHIE: I want to tell you a story.

28. INT. AUSTRIAN HOTEL. DAY

A long marble balustrade gleams over a forlorn hotel lobby, which shows signs of decay. A waiter, who has been loading fallen plaster on to a wheelbarrow, is now sitting in a chair, reading a newspaper. No one else is in sight.

SOPHIE: (*Voice over*) It must have been the first summer after the war. My mother and I went back to the hotel where we had always spent our Augusts. Maybe you know the place – the Toplitz at Bad Gastein? Anyway, father stayed behind in Vienna.

29. INT. FREUD'S ROOM. DAY

YOUNG SOPHIE *is lying on the couch, huddled in her coat.*

She is continuing her story.

YOUNG SOPHIE: The place had been used as a hospital. Soldiers had carved their names on the banisters. Most of the rooms were still closed up. The people I remembered from before the war – the gardeners, the enormous French chefs – they were all gone.

30. INT. HOTEL. DAY

A porter, carrying suitcases, struggles up the lobby steps and across the foyer. His footsteps echo in the empty grandeur of the all but deserted hotel.

SOPHIE: (*Voice over; amused by the memory*) At dinner they served up boiled potatoes and cabbage – on huge silver platters! They kept up appearances in all the wreckage. (*Pause.*) It was August, but the place was damp. I felt chilled. That was when my childhood ended.

31. INT. ALEXANDER'S APARTMENT. DAY

SOPHIE *stands by the window, lost in thought. She looks across at* ALEXANDER. *He is sitting at the table, absorbed in his own thoughts.*

32. INT. FREUD'S ROOM. DAY

YOUNG SOPHIE *is sitting on the couch. She draws up her knees to make herself more comfortable, and she smiles.*

YOUNG SOPHIE: After about two weeks my mother and I went to the station to meet my father. I walked ahead of her down the platform. It was crowded with refugees. There were still soldiers everywhere. Piles of luggage. Then I saw her. Anna. She was wearing a coral-pink dress and a grey scarf. (*Pause.*) She shone! Everything around her seemed to fade away.

33. EXT. RAILWAY STATION. DAY

ANNA'*s face in profile. She is half-smiling, a touch of irony in her face. The first impression is of beauty; then her expression reveals that there is something more than beauty here: power and intelligence.*

34. INT. FREUD'S ROOM. DAY

YOUNG SOPHIE: She was standing on the platform waiting for the porter to cope with her luggage and talking to the man who was with her. She was joking with him . . . toying with him.

35. INT. ALEXANDER'S APARTMENT. DAY

SOPHIE *is musing; then, with a sudden movement of her wrist:*

SOPHIE: She touched his cheek with her glove. Just a flick. Like that.

36. INT. FREUD'S ROOM. DAY

YOUNG SOPHIE *is still perched on the couch, her face full of pleasure. She turns and, almost falling, lies back on the cushions.*

YOUNG SOPHIE: I completely forgot about my father. He came up behind me and tapped me on the shoulder. (*Mimicking slightly*) 'Remember me?' – with that icy politeness he has when he's angry. 'I see you've been daydreaming again.' But he was eyeing Anna.

37. INT. ALEXANDER'S APARTMENT. DAY

SOPHIE *is again standing by the window. She is reliving the moment.* ALEXANDER *is at the table, staring into the vase of flowers.*

SOPHIE: Anna turned. She'd heard him. She looked at me. I blushed. Like a schoolgirl.

38. INT. FREUD'S ROOM. DAY

YOUNG SOPHIE *is lying on the couch. She looks distraught, her face very white among the richly coloured fabrics.*

YOUNG SOPHIE: They all talk – my mother, my father, *you* too – as if I had some disease. *I'm in love with a woman. That*'s why I'm here.

FREUD: (*Quietly*) You are not here because you're in love. You are here because you tried to kill yourself.

39. INT. FREUD'S ROOM. DAY

YOUNG ALEXANDER *is lying on the couch, still muffled in his greatcoat, staring upwards, talking softly.*

YOUNG ALEXANDER: I meet her in the storeroom of the café after work. She washes dishes there. A big, red-faced woman. Large breasts. (*Pause.*) Strong. (*Pause.*) The smell . . . of cabbage . . . (*Self-mocking*)

Just my type. Nina knows nothing, of course. I cannot understand myself . . . I want to see . . . I want to see . . . (*Loses himself in fantasy, unable or unwilling to conceal his arousal.*) Mmmm . . . that's it . . . Shake, you bitch . . . That's it . . . (*Whispers*) What a disgusting woman!
(*Silence.* YOUNG ALEXANDER's *eyes are wide, dark, unblinking.*)

40. INT. ALEXANDER'S APARTMENT. DAY

ALEXANDER's *eyes fill the screen. They are deep-set, almost sunken, very lined and tired.* SOPHIE *is watching him; he appears to be staring into space.*

SOPHIE: Mr Scherbatov . . .

(ALEXANDER *turns towards her as if woken suddenly.*

He looks at her sheepishly. SOPHIE *is amused, not angry. She sits down at the table, opposite* ALEXANDER.) You listen just like my husband. Not at all. (ALEXANDER *perks up and looks inquiringly at her.*)

ALEXANDER: You have a husband?

SOPHIE: For twelve years. No longer. (*Pause. As if speaking to herself, very quietly*) I seem to have lived too long. (*She gets up from the table.*) When I got married, I thought, now I'm going to find out. With a woman, you're . . . (*Searching for the words*) with yourself; with a man . . . I thought, now I'll see . . .

41. INT. HOTEL. NIGHT

ANNA, *wearing a long silver ball gown, stands at the entrance to the hotel dining room. She is waiting for someone. She*

moves, back and forth, at the door. This is not impatience but a confident, though gentle, display. She is magnificent, assured; as the camera rests on her, it is worldliness as well as beauty that compels attention.

42. INT. ALEXANDER'S APARTMENT. DAY

SOPHIE: That first evening Anna swept past our table in the dining room. She was on the arm of a man. The man I had seen her with at the station. (*Pauses over the memory.*) My father said, 'You mustn't stare at that girl. It is indecent.' (*Smiles; then softly to herself*) Indecent.

(ALEXANDER *is sitting at the table. He has again sunk into a reverie, his eyes half-closed. He blinks, as if waking up. He looks about himself, wondering what to do to make amends for not listening.*)

43. INT. FREUD'S ROOM. DAY

YOUNG SOPHIE *lies back on the couch. Her clothes suggest warmer weather: a blouse of light material and no overcoat. She is playing with a pendant on a silver chain. Her eyes are narrowed, and her head is angled slightly: she is listening intently to* FREUD.

FREUD: Why do you think I share your father's morality? It is the logic of your love, its roots in the past, not its morality, that concerns you and me . . .

(YOUNG SOPHIE *moves her eyes as if to look towards the man sitting behind her. She half-smiles: a flicker of scepticism.*)

Who *is* Anna, Sophie? What does she represent?

44. INT. HOTEL. NIGHT

ANNA *walks into the grand, glittering but almost empty dining room. A man, obviously expecting her to join him at his table, rises from his chair to greet her.*

45. INT. ALEXANDER'S APARTMENT. DAY

SOPHIE *is again standing at the window of the apartment. She glances towards* ALEXANDER *at the table, then looks up at the lace curtains.*

SOPHIE: That night I couldn't sleep. My parents were in the next room. I lay there, listening to my father snoring, turning in the bed, the springs creaking. I thought of Anna somewhere nearby, with her lover . . .

(*She shudders and folds her arms tightly, as if to shield herself against the memory.*)

46. INT. HOTEL. NIGHT

YOUNG SOPHIE *is standing at a french window. She stares out, her arms wrapped around herself. A white lace curtain billows in front of her.*

47. INT. ALEXANDER'S APARTMENT. DAY

ALEXANDER *is in his tiny kitchen, making tea.* SOPHIE *is standing at the entrance to the kitchen alcove.*

SOPHIE: (*Musing*) When I was 18 I thought getting old would be like walking down to the beach for a swim, in the dark. Dropping your hat and glasses, your bag. Leaving your clothes in a trail down to the edge. And then just slipping into the sea. But it's not like that.

(*The noise of crockery ceases.* ALEXANDER *is listening now.*)

You don't want to let go of anything. You cling to it all. You want everything as much as you ever did . . .

(ALEXANDER *comes out of the kitchen carrying a tray on which there are a kettle, tea glasses in silver holders and slices of lemon on a plate. He squeezes past* SOPHIE, *puts the tray on the table and gets a bowl of dark, crystalline sugar from a cupboard beside the* chaise-longue.)

ALEXANDER: I heard a good joke. A woman meets her friend, who has a new baby. 'What a lovely child,' she says. The mother replies, 'Wait till you see his photograph!'

(*He chuckles, then looks up at* SOPHIE.)

We Russians make the only tea worth drinking.

(*He pours a cup, drops in a slice of lemon and hands it to* SOPHIE.)

Do you have a dog in New York?

SOPHIE: A dog?

ALEXANDER: When you live alone . . .

(*He looks at her. She looks at him with a smile and a tiny shrug. She resists; he persists.*) Do you live alone? A pet perhaps?

SOPHIE: You are hopeless.

ALEXANDER: (*Shrugging and turning away*) Humph . . . They don't allow dogs in this building. (*He sits by the tea things looking glum and blank. The phone rings. He doesn't answer. He looks at it balefully.* SOPHIE *moves towards the window, watching him sardonically while she sips her tea. The phone is still ringing.*)

A vulgar woman. She lives here. (*Points to floor.*) Number 27. (*Elaborate stage whisper*) She knows you're here! How do I let myself get attached to them? And she is a communist. Or so she says. Disgusting, really . . . (*The phone stops ringing.* SOPHIE, *now by the window, gives him an impatient glance. Her arms are folded. She looks out of the window, down into the courtyard below.*

Footsteps echo on the cobblestones; voices rise to the window.)

48. EXT. REVOLUTIONARY RUSSIA. DAY

Black-and-white newsreel images: a platoon of the Red cavalry; the roar of a Red Army song; Bolshevik soldiers

advance along a railway siding; Cossacks sweep across the plains.

49. INT. HOTEL CONSERVATORY. DAY

ANNA *is sitting in the conservatory in bright early morning sunlight, sipping her coffee and reading a newspaper.* YOUNG SOPHIE *walks in, sees* ANNA, *hesitates.* ANNA *holds up the newspaper.*

ANNA: (*Mocking*) The Bolshevik hordes will be knocking on the gates of Vienna any day now.

(*She moves another chair towards her table and gestures to* YOUNG SOPHIE *to sit down.* ANNA *throws aside her newspaper and pours* YOUNG SOPHIE *a cup of coffee.*)

I remember this place before the war. (*She is amused, pleased at the hotel's dilapidated condition.*)

YOUNG SOPHIE: So do I.

ANNA: It's falling apart. Just like Austria!

(*She makes a gesture of pretend dismay, then laughs. A young Viennese aristocrat enters the conservatory to join* ANNA *for breakfast. He nods stiffly and ungraciously at* YOUNG SOPHIE.)

Poor Reinhardt is in mourning for the monarchy (*In a sarcastic whisper*) Wake up, Reinhardt!

(YOUNG SOPHIE *and* ANNA *laugh.*)

50. INT. FREUD'S ROOM. DAY

YOUNG SOPHIE *is on the couch, slumped, arms folded, tense with indignation.*

YOUNG SOPHIE: Why don't you just come out and say it? She lives off men.

FREUD: There is a word for that.

YOUNG SOPHIE: (*Coldly*) Your word, not mine. (*Looks away contemptuously*) You sound like my father.

FREUD: You have to recognize who she is.

YOUNG SOPHIE: (*Very sure; no irony*) I do. (*Long pause.*) She says that ordinary people, real people, will change the world. She knows there is something to live for.

51. INT. ALEXANDER'S APARTMENT. DAY

SOPHIE *is standing at the window as if her attention were still fixed on the courtyard below. She turns to* ALEXANDER. *He is sitting glumly at the table. He has not poured any tea for himself.* SOPHIE *comes towards him, speaking with the fervent voice of her younger self.*

SOPHIE: You can't imagine: around the dinner table at home, father would go on and on about our precious savings and the Bolshevik menace. And here she was, in that beautiful suit and that blouse of hers – someone who didn't talk as if the whole world was about to come to an end.

(ALEXANDER *looks up at her from the table, an indignant expression on his face.*)

ALEXANDER: But it had!

(SOPHIE *turns away from him. She is still wrapped up in her memory of* ANNA.)

SOPHIE: She didn't give a damn what anyone thought . . .

ALEXANDER: How can you talk like this? Of course the world had come to an end! Before, they had treated me like a . . . like a prince. (*He speaks without pathos, simply asserting a fact.*) They took everything! It *was* the end of the world!

(SOPHIE *raises her glass of tea in an ironic toast.*)

SOPHIE: Here's to the end of the world. (*She drinks a brisk mouthful.*)

It was the end of my world too. (*Bitterly*) Only you knew it. And I didn't.

(*She sits at the table, facing* ALEXANDER. *She looks straight at him. He leans away from her. She shouts at him.*) I was a socialist, Alexander. (*Pause. She sits back, becomes calmer.*)

I still am. Even in America. Though the word has changed . . . Do you know what it meant in 1920, in a bourgeois family with a war profiteer for a father? To be a socialist? No, you wouldn't. That old world of yours had me by the throat . . . and Anna could see it.

(*She looks away from him and almost whispers:*)

Though God knows she had more reason to want to smash up the old world than I did.

ALEXANDER: You were just a girl. What could you know about socialism?

SOPHIE: (*Softly, wearily*) What could *you* know about socialism? With your *dessiatin*, your estates? (*To herself*) About being a woman?

52. INT. FREUD'S ROOM. DAY

YOUNG SOPHIE *is lying on the couch. She is full of energy.*

YOUNG SOPHIE: After breakfast in the conservatory we spent the day together. When the man Anna was with came down to breakfast, she told him that she thought he should go back to Vienna. Just like that. There was a scene. (*Smiles.*) It was quite funny. (*Pause.*) After that we were inseparable. For that whole week, we swam, played tennis, walked in the gardens at night. My father said, 'You are making a spectacle of yourself. She is years older than you.' (*Sardonically*) As if that was the problem.

53. EXT. HOTEL BALCONY. NIGHT

ANNA *and* YOUNG SOPHIE *are standing side by side on the balcony, looking out at the hotel garden. It is a very dark, moonless night. Behind them glow the yellow lights of hotel rooms.* YOUNG SOPHIE *points to the pendant that* ANNA *is wearing.* ANNA *removes it and gently fastens it round* YOUNG SOPHIE'*s neck.* YOUNG SOPHIE, *overjoyed, kisses her on the cheek.*

FREUD: (*Voice over; soft, exploratory*) I want to suggest something. You have been acting out the masculine part with Anna. It is as if . . . she were . . . your mother.

YOUNG SOPHIE: (*Voice over; laughs incredulously*) My mother? My mother doesn't care about me. She lives for my father.

FREUD: (*Voice over*) Exactly.

54. INT. FREUD'S ROOM. DAY

YOUNG SOPHIE *is lying back on the couch but stares angrily across the room, away from* FREUD.

YOUNG SOPHIE: Exactly what?

FREUD: You are acting out what life denies you. You are a woman who would rather die than admit your love for your father.

YOUNG SOPHIE: My father disgusts me!

55. INT. VIENNA OPERA, 1920S. NIGHT

Black-and-white newsreel: the Viennese bourgeoisie, in top hats and evening dress, throngs the foyer of the Opera House. An orchestra is tuning up.

YOUNG SOPHIE: (*Voice over*) He is a vulture, my father. He descends on the battlefields. He buys up the uniforms, the guns, the scrap metal. Sells them all in Romania or somewhere. He never tells us.

56. EXT. RUSSIA, 1920S. DAY

Black-and-white images: lines of families with their ragged possessions at a railroad siding; an air of mute submission; close-up of a thin, wide-eyed boy staring out from a refugee camp of the past, desolate yet without reproach.

YOUNG SOPHIE: (*Voice over*) I once asked him where our money came from. He said, 'I will not discuss it at the dinner table.' He actually said that. (*Hisses the words*) *So when will you discuss it?*

57. INT. AUSTRIAN HOTEL. DAY

A self-confident Viennese bourgeois of the 1920s is at a table in the dining room, eating a large breakfast: eggs, cold meat, rolls. The face is arrogant, stern and sensual. This is SOPHIE*'s father. He looks up. He sees* ANNA. *She is walking past the dining room doorway. She pauses. He stares, glares, then a glimmer of lust. He resumes his breakfast.*

FREUD: (*Voice over*) It is not your father *now* that you desire. The father you love is the father of your infancy. (*Pause.*) The forgotten father . . . You think you want Anna. You also want your father.

58. INT. FREUD'S ROOM. DAY

On the couch YOUNG SOPHIE *cranes her head upwards as if trying to look* FREUD *in the eye. She smiles.*

YOUNG SOPHIE: (*Bantering*) So I am a divided creature? With two natures?

FREUD: (*Quietly*) It has nothing to do with natures.

(YOUNG SOPHIE*'s smile disappears. She returns to her*

normal position on the couch, staring, eyes narrowed. A long silence.)

YOUNG SOPHIE: (*Stubbornly*) I love Anna.

FREUD: (*Wearily conscious that he is repeating himself*) But who *is* she?

59. INT. ALEXANDER'S APARTMENT. DAY

SOPHIE *is sitting at the table. She has reached the climax of her story; she is tense and in pain.* ALEXANDER *is sitting opposite her.*

SOPHIE: The last night came. She was returning to Vienna the next day. We walked in the gardens after dark. She kissed me and went up to her room. She didn't say a word. I waited till my parents were asleep. (*Pause.*) I was in my nightgown. I knocked softly on the door and went in . . .

60. INT. HOTEL BEDROOM. NIGHT

ANNA *is in bed. She is sitting up. Her long hair cascades on to her shoulders; her face is lit by a candle on a bedside table. She looks up. There is a hint of a smile on her lips.*

61. INT. ALEXANDER'S APARTMENT. DAY

SOPHIE: I had never seen her hair down before . . . on the pillows . . . auburn . . . (*She stares up at the ceiling. She shakes her head, as if to say, 'Why am I telling you all this?'*)
She said, 'I have been happy with you . . .'
(*Pause.* SOPHIE *looks across at* ALEXANDER. *He is watching her, suddenly full of curiosity. She looks away.*)

62. INT. FREUD'S ROOM. DAY

YOUNG SOPHIE *is sitting with her feet on the couch. She has been crying.*

FREUD: So you became lovers.

YOUNG SOPHIE: What does it matter?

FREUD: (*Mild, even friendly*) You might have made your choice. We would not now be talking of cures.

YOUNG SOPHIE: (*With irritation*) Cures! No . . . (*Pause; then softly and definitely*) No, we didn't.

(*A silence.* YOUNG SOPHIE *is very still.*)

FREUD: (*Quietly*) No.

63. INT. HOTEL BEDROOM. NIGHT

YOUNG SOPHIE *turns from the white curtains that hang in front of the french window. She approaches* ANNA, *who is lying in her hotel bed.* ANNA'*s nightgown is undone; the sheet and covers are pulled back; she is almost naked.* ANNA *smiles.* YOUNG SOPHIE *sits beside her.* ANNA *takes*

her hands and guides them down her breasts, on to her belly. ANNA *is pregnant.* YOUNG SOPHIE'*s hands explore the surface of the skin. There is an erotic exploration, yet the hands move as if to find the palpable life beneath the skin.* ANNA *and* YOUNG SOPHIE *kiss gently, then with passion.*

64. INT. ALEXANDER'S APARTMENT. DAY

ALEXANDER *and* SOPHIE *are still sitting opposite one another at the table.*

ALEXANDER: You made love?

SOPHIE: (*Staring upward, angry*) No. Yes. (*Looks at him sharply and shrugs.*) What does it matter?

ALEXANDER: (*Vaguely*) I never knew any homosexual women in Russia . . .

SOPHIE: (*Quiet but angry*) That was the happiest night of my life. Why did I think you would understand? (*Her voice begins to rise.*) For that one night I spent years explaining myself. I thought you might at least begin to understand *why* I fought with him, why I *had* to. But you don't understand, do you?
(*She leans towards him. He looks away.*) You paid him to listen all those years about your women and your bowels. But *you* never listened to anyone. (*Bitterly*) Did he tell you to listen?

ALEXANDER: (*Distractedly*) *He* listened. *I* talked. And the Red Army marched into Odessa. Rome burned; Nero fiddled. At least he made music! (*He begins to drift.*) One thing he did say to me about the war: he said we have the wrong attitude to death. Twenty million dead . . . What *was* he talking about?
(SOPHIE, *irritated by* ALEXANDER'*s drifting, leans very close to him.*)

SOPHIE: (*Spitting the words out quietly but intensely*) He was a good listener. I hated him. But he threaded every word, like pearls, on a necklace. Those theories . . . But *you*.

(ALEXANDER's *face is frozen, staring straight ahead.*) Something knocked the stuffing out of you. The Revolution. Your father's dogs. Wars. Someone ran you over and left you for dead. (*Fighting back tears*) There isn't anything left of you, is there? *Is there*? (*She pauses but she cannot control her despair.*) He's gone. Anna's gone. And now you've gone.

65. INT. HOTEL BEDROOM. MORNING

ANNA *and* YOUNG SOPHIE *are lying across the bed.* ANNA *is asleep in* YOUNG SOPHIE's *arms.* YOUNG SOPHIE *is awake, watching the dawn light begin to filter through the white curtains. She strokes* ANNA's *hair.*

66. INT. ALEXANDER'S APARTMENT. DAY

SOPHIE *and* ALEXANDER *across the table.* SOPHIE *is weeping helplessly.*

SOPHIE: Why did I come back? Why?

(ALEXANDER *is watching her. They sit for a long moment walled away in their solitude. Very slowly* ALEXANDER *reaches out and takes the smouldering cigarette butt from* SOPHIE's *fingers. Then he reaches across the table and tentatively, gently – as if he were experimenting – strokes* SOPHIE's *hair. The gesture is brief. She shakes him off. He hands her a handkerchief. She takes it. He removes his hand and sits motionless with both hands folded on the table in front of him. Then he gets up and walks to the mirror, the bric-à-brac and the family photographs. He picks up a portrait of* NINA *in a silver frame. He tilts it, scrutinizes it, as if seeing this photograph of a sad face for the first time. When he begins to speak it is in a distant voice but unlike the distracted and irritable tones of before.* SOPHIE *looks up at him, angry and hurt. Noisily she lights another cigarette. She takes the monologue that starts as another*

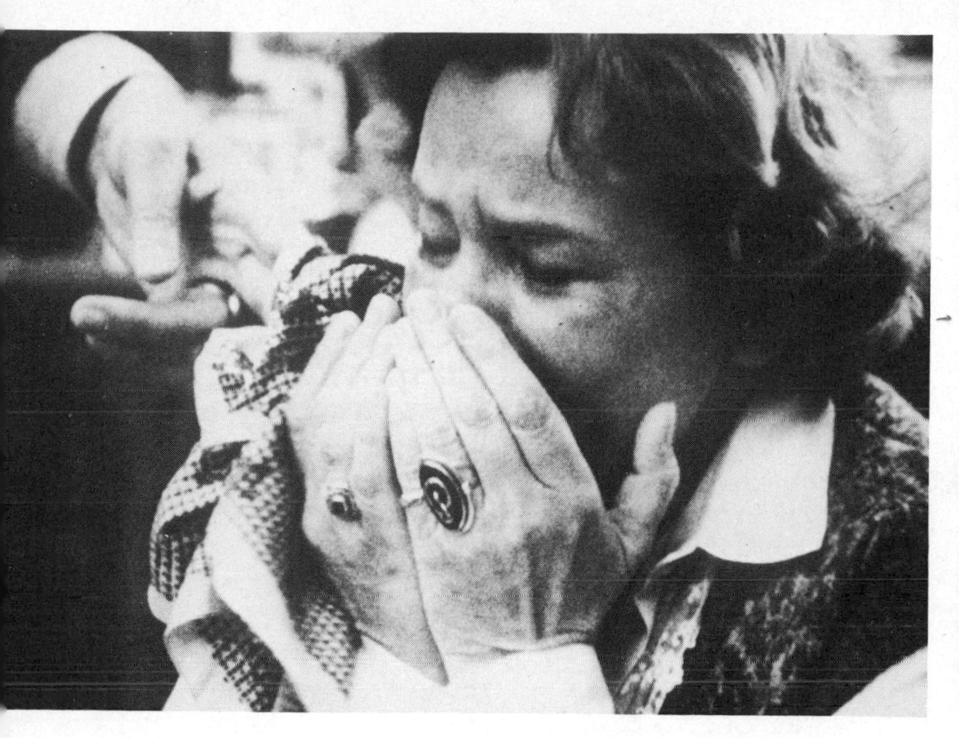

sign that he cannot even listen to her grief. But as he continues, she realizes that he is trying to respond to what she has said – by sharing an important and painful memory of his own.)

ALEXANDER: They were all against her: mother, father, the doctors, my sister. My father said, 'Is she some kind of brothel-keeper or something?' I said, 'She is nothing of the kind. She owns a respectable boarding house. The best families in Odessa stay there. *I* stay there.'

67. EXT. RUSSIAN FOREST IN WINTER. DAY

Black-and-white home movie: droshkis and horses gather in a clearing in front of a log-built dacha. The woods are blanketed in snow.

68. INT. ALEXANDER'S APARTMENT. DAY

ALEXANDER: I took her back to the estate, you know. The winter of 1914. January. There was hunting. They all thought she'd never manage – (*Mimicking*) 'little Austrian commoner' – in the cold. I bundled her up in the droshki. Our coachman took care . . . I can bring it all back any time I like. (*Narrows his eyes: almost a parody of remembering.*)

69. EXT. RUSSIAN STEPPE IN WINTER. DAY

Black-and-white home movie: men on horseback lead hunting dogs on leashes along the edge of a pine forest. A wolf hunt is gathering pace. A wolf scampers across a flat white field. The dogs are let loose; horsemen gallop behind. The dogs bring the wolf down. A huntsman leaps from his horse to make the kill.

ALEXANDER: (*Voice over*) We flushed him out of the woods in to the field. We let the dogs go . . . I was on him . . . I was on him. Sergei and father were far behind! The droshkis caught up with us. I went to her. She was blue with cold . . . I took off her muff and blew on her hands and rubbed them . . . She pulled away. She said, 'You've got blood all over you.'

70. INT. ALEXANDER'S APARTMENT. DAY

ALEXANDER *stands at the mirror, a hurt expression on his face.* SOPHIE *watches him uneasily.*

ALEXANDER: (*His voice now full of disappointment*) She said, 'I want to go home.'

(*He pauses, looks at his hands, shrugs.*)

We returned to Vienna in the spring.

(ALEXANDER *makes a gesture of helplessness, then walks round the table to the other side of the room. He turns to look at* SOPHIE *sitting at the table, her face still red with tears.*)

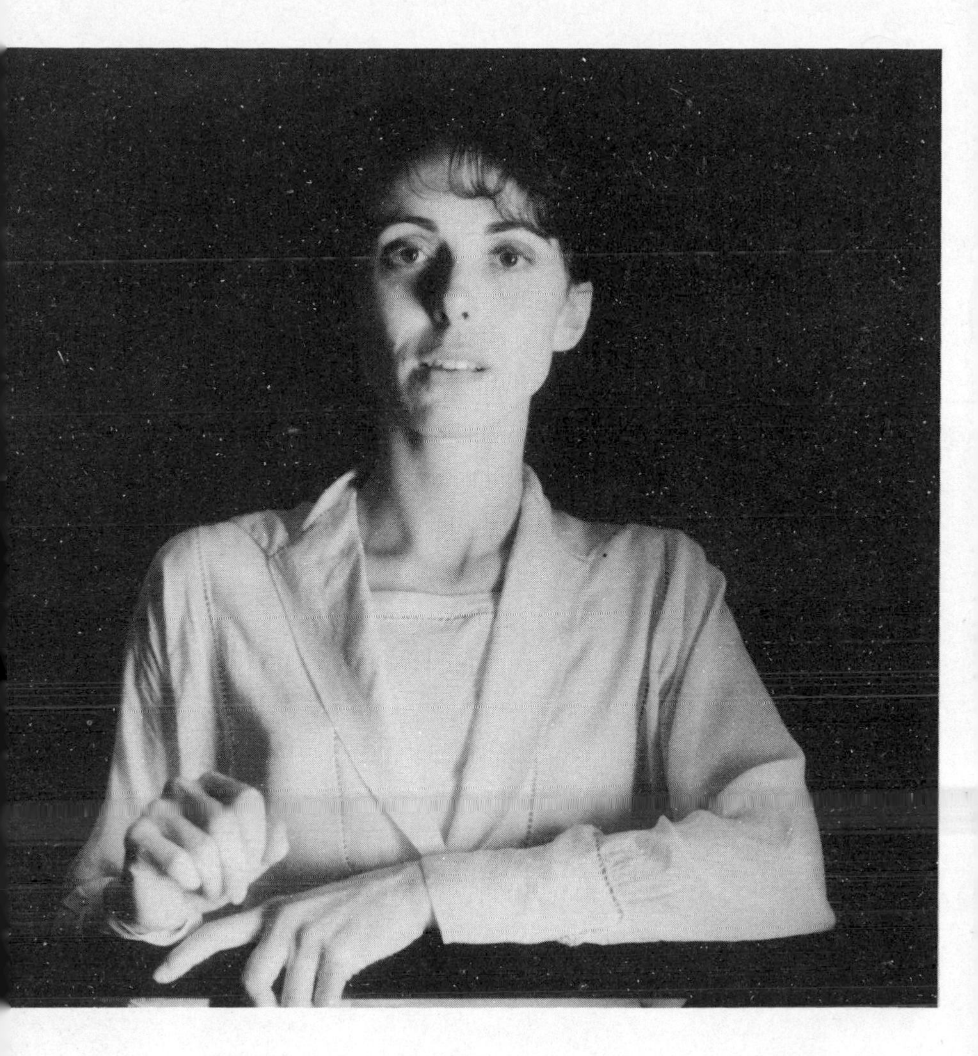

I went back to Odessa, to persuade them to let me marry Nina. It was summer. The soil was parched. The dust! My brother Sergei blew cigar smoke in my face. He said, 'So you've decided to throw yourself away on one of those sluts of yours, I hear.' I said, 'She's not a slut, Sergei.'

71. EXT. RUSSIA. DAY

A black-and-white photograph, 1910: a grand open-air lunch party. The guests sit around a huge oval table. They are turning in their seats to pose for the camera. Cut to black-and-white newsreel, 1916: aristocratic couples, dressed as if for a wedding, step through a doorway and past the camera. It is as if they were plunging off the face of the earth.

ALEXANDER: (*Voice over; a strange mimicry of different voices*) 'Aren't you well, Alexander?' 'Won't you be off to serve the Tsar?' 'My son takes after me – with his nervous condition.'

72. EXT. FIRST WORLD WAR BATTLEFIELD. DAY

Smoke and dust drift across a desolate no-man's-land. A solitary pine tree is the only living thing to be seen. This tree is now the gunners' target: shells explode around it. Clouds of smoke and dust drift across a hillside.

73. INT. ALEXANDER'S APARTMENT. DAY

SOPHIE: What are you *talking* about?

ALEXANDER: War was declared. I was trapped on the estate. I couldn't get back to Nina. I couldn't resume my treatment. There weren't even letters between us – not for three years. I couldn't even fight. (*Muttering to himself*) Someone had to stay with mother. (*He sits down facing* SOPHIE.)
You see, my brothers were all killed. And when my father came home, he couldn't talk. He was silent. For months. And then the Revolution . . .
(*Protesting*) It was the war . . . It would never have happened . . .

SOPHIE: (*Impatient*) But . . .

ALEXANDER: What do you know? I was there . . . the peasants . . .

SOPHIE: They would have cut your throat . . .

ALEXANDER: (*Waving her argument aside, impatient and increasingly desperate*) I thought, I must get out of here.

74. EXT. RUSSIAN REVOLUTION. DAY

Black-and-white newsreel images: the façade of the Winter Palace in the snow; icicles hang from broken windows; a crowd storms the gates; revolutionaries march past carrying banners.

ALEXANDER: (*Voice over*) It was June 1917. No one had manhandled us. (*Pleading*) There was enough food. (*Miserably*) I thought I could go. I thought everyone

would be all right. I said, 'I'll be back in November, with Nina. I'll finish my treatment. You'll see. Everything will be all right.'

75. INT. ALEXANDER'S APARTMENT. DAY

ALEXANDER: (*Muttering*) What a disaster.

SOPHIE: (*Gently*) No one ever thinks it will happen to them. (*Pause. Then, as if* SOPHIE *had not spoken:*)

ALEXANDER: I never saw my mother again.

76. INT. STAIRWELL. DAY

NINA, *drawn and pale, is staring down at* ALEXANDER. *As his footsteps approach, she covers her face with her hand in anguish and turns away.*

77. INT. ALEXANDER'S APARTMENT. DAY

ALEXANDER: Nina was on the landing. She just stared at me, and then she burst into tears. 'You've changed, you've changed,' she kept saying. (*Distantly, as if thinking out loud*) But *she* had changed. So thin. Destitute. The place was filthy. She was . . . dying of neglect. I had neglected her.

(*He gets up rather abruptly and walks across the room, away from the table, away from* SOPHIE. *Then he speaks with surprising decisiveness*:)

I realized we must be married at once. I wanted to marry . . .

(*Then he walks around the table, past* SOPHIE *and behind a screen that hides another room. He is out of sight. The noise of a cupboard door opening, hangers being moved along a rail, the cupboard door closing. From behind the screen*:) Nina said, 'What will we live on? I've lost the house. And you? What do you know how to do?' (*He reappears from behind the screen, dressed in an old, frayed tail-coat with huge wing lapels: an impeccably tailored garment now on its last legs.*)

I said, 'I am going to become a waiter.' This is all I had. With my shirt, my studs and my patent leather shoes, of course.

(*Takes a step towards* SOPHIE, *smoothing the lapels of the old dinner jacket, then he stands very still, lost in the memory of what it meant to him, this tail-coat.* SOPHIE *looks at him, smiles, is embarrassed by a need to laugh, turns away.* ALEXANDER *does not notice her reactions.*)

It still fits me, doesn't it? There are some things they can never take away from you.

(*Slowly his self-absorption ebbs away. He looks across at* SOPHIE. *He seems puzzled.*) Where was I?

SOPHIE: (*Cheerfully*) You were a waiter.

ALEXANDER: (*Trying to pick up the thread again*) Ah yes,

I became a waiter. You know, he treated me for nothing. For months. He said, 'You have nothing. I have nothing. So let's forget about money for a while.'

78. INT. FREUD'S ROOM. DAY

YOUNG ALEXANDER *lies on the couch, muffled in a greatcoat, shivering occasionally. His face is very white and full of self-absorption.*

ALEXANDER: (*Voice over*) We went further and further back . . . my father's dogs . . . mother waking up in the garden, not knowing who I was. Further and further back . . . rolling over and over down the hill with my sister . . . at the lake . . .

79. INT. FREUD'S ROOM. DAY

YOUNG ALEXANDER *relaxes, looks round in* FREUD's *direction.*

YOUNG ALEXANDER: My sister . . . she is the brilliant one. There is nothing she can't play (*Drifting*) . . . Tanaev . . . Scriabin . . . She said to me, 'The trouble with you is that you are always waiting for someone to come and save you.'

FREUD: Where is she now?

YOUNG ALEXANDER: I don't know. She is lost . . .

FREUD: What do you mean?

YOUNG ALEXANDER: She was in the battle for Novorossisk, a nurse . . .

FREUD: So, she would have been evacuated by the British fleet?

YOUNG ALEXANDER: No. You misunderstand. She was . . . not with us.

FREUD: She . . .

YOUNG ALEXANDER: With them . . . the Bolsheviks. (*Ironically*) She believed in salvation after all. How *could* she?

80. EXT. RUSSIAN ESTATE. DAY

ALEXANDER'S SISTER, *holding the three Borzois, watching her brother fencing. She laughs.* YOUNG ALEXANDER *rips off his fencing mask, lunges at her, his face twisted with fury. He thrusts the rapier at her: the point touches her throat. She does not flinch but looks down at the rapier point. She just laughs at him.*

81. INT. ALEXANDER'S APARTMENT. DAY

ALEXANDER *and* SOPHIE *are sitting at the table. The silver-framed photograph of* NINA *is at* SOPHIE'*s elbow. She looks at it.*

ALEXANDER: We talked. I gave him what he wanted. But I kept saying, 'When can I marry my Nina?' He said,

'Stop talking about your blessed Nina.'

SOPHIE: You needed his permission to marry?

ALEXANDER: That was the rule. One must agree to the treatment. The *contract*.

SOPHIE: (*Indignant*) Why did you let him?

(ALEXANDER, *head bent, looks at* SOPHIE *sheepishly*.)

ALEXANDER: I was unsure. I needed to make up my

mind . . . about Nina. I depended on him . . .

SOPHIE: (*Incredulous*) You needed pyschoanalysis for this?

ALEXANDER: He said there was a neurosis . . . (*A sudden imitation, almost a parody, of* FREUD) 'Unresolved transference residues.' Dreams . . . he said my dreams were very important.

SOPHIE: (*Sardonic*) So he got the dreams. And you got your Nina.
(*Pause.*)

ALEXANDER: He saw her worth . . . (*Smiling faintly*) He said to me, when the treatment was over, 'Bravo, Alexander, you have made the breakthrough to the woman.' (*Haunted, softly*) The breakthrough to the woman . . .
(*Long pause. Then* ALEXANDER *gets up, crosses the room, stops, turns and looks back towards* SOPHIE. *She is absorbed in her own thoughts.*) We were married in 1920.

82. EXT. VIENNA. DAY

Black-and-white newsreel images: Ringstrasse in the 1920s; the ebullient Vienna of ALEXANDER's *days as a waiter; busy but not crowded streets; young people wave from open-topped cars. Then a newsvendor on another street – now it is the 1930s. He waves a newspaper. Then a troop carrier: paramilitaries leap out on to a side road, Nazis are rounding up their opponents. Then back to the Ringstrasse, 1934: a densely packed crowd presses against a cordon of police.*

ALEXANDER: (*Voice over*) We were all right for a time. I worked at the café. We went to the movies . . . There was trouble later. Brownshirts . . . fights in the streets . . . Once, right in the middle of the café, a terrible fight. I remember they pulled a man out of his chair. And threw him into the street. A regular customer. I don't know what happened to him. It was better not to ask.

83. INT. ALEXANDER'S APARTMENT. DAY

ALEXANDER *is standing across the room, beside the screen. He looks helpless, marooned.*

ALEXANDER: (*Pleading*) We were happy. We found this apartment . . . We lived in it . . . together.
(SOPHIE *has taken a compact out of her handbag. She stands now, toying with her hair, putting on lipstick. She is impatient with* ALEXANDER*'s attempt to escape his times.*)

SOPHIE: I used to go to the newsreels in New York. I remember they had one on Vienna, after '34. They had bombarded the workers' apartments. And again in '38. I used to sit there in the audience thinking, I'm going to see her in the crowd, I'm going to see her . . . But you never see anyone in newsreels.

84. EXT. VIENNA. DAY

Black-and-white newsreel: the 1930s. A line of mounted police confronts a demonstration. A terrified woman runs across the street. A police horse stampedes a demonstrator. Police batons are being used fiercely against demonstrators. The scene is violent, yet also somehow stagey, unreal.

SOPHIE: (*Voice over*) It just passed you by, didn't it? The politics of it. Every day I read about the arrests, the marches. Didn't you *do* anything?

ALEXANDER: (*Voice over*) You weren't there.

SOPHIE: (*Voice over*) They were arresting people every day.

ALEXANDER: (*Voice over*) You weren't there. You ran away.

85. INT. ALEXANDER'S APARTMENT. DAY

SOPHIE *snaps her compact shut. She is stung by* ALEXANDER*'s accusation.*

SOPHIE: What did Nina say?

ALEXANDER: Nina? She said there are times when people should make themselves invisible.
(*He walks across the room, past* SOPHIE, *struggling with*

a rising violence in himself.)
We tried to be invisible.
(*He suddenly swings round as if to attack* SOPHIE, *then checks himself.*)
I'm going to tell you something . . . My headaches began to return . . . Symptoms . . . I went back to Berggasse. A woman, one of his daughters, came to the door. I said, 'Do you remember me? I need his help. It is coming back again . . .' She said, 'My father is sick. He cannot help you.'

86. INT. FREUD'S ROOM. DAY

YOUNG ALEXANDER *is lying, white-faced, on the couch. His eyes are filled with despair.*

FREUD: Alexander, for you there are women who are your sisters . . .

YOUNG ALEXANDER: And there are women who are shit!

FREUD: Women you pay . . . and women too good to pay, too good to touch.

87. INT. ALEXANDER'S APARTMENT. DAY

ALEXANDER *and* SOPHIE *are standing nose to nose. Her face is full of uneasy apprehension. As* ALEXANDER *speaks his next lines, her expression gives way to a mixture of pity and revulsion.*

ALEXANDER: (*Mimicking*) Yes, there are women who are your sisters. (*Picking up his own voice in a rage*) And there are women who are shit! (*Pause.*) There was one in the café. She washed the dishes there. It was always hot in the kitchen. She was big, covered with sweat. I would hand her the plates through the hatch. (*Mimicking savagely*) 'Keep your hands off me', and then, quick as a wink, 'Meet me in the storeroom after.' (*Beginning to rage in his despair*) Why did I go to her? Why? In the storeroom, among the sacks of

flour, the crates of whisky. Bang, bang, bang! (*Mimicking again*) 'Come on! You Russians are useless! Do what you like. You're paying.' She would stand on a chair, waving herself at me. (*There is a flicker of lust in his rage.*) She said, 'We're all in the muck together.' But *she* was the muck! *She* was the shit!

(ALEXANDER *has reached a frenzy of desperate anger. He lunges towards* SOPHIE, *seizing her with one hand on the throat, his other hand grasping the back of her head. For a moment* SOPHIE *remains immobilized, calculating how best to deal with this attack, wondering how dangerous it really is. Then, with a very strong twist of her head, she pulls away from his hands.*)

SOPHIE: Sit down. It's all over.

ALEXANDER: (*Between clenched teeth*) It's not over at all.

(ALEXANDER *turns away from* SOPHIE. *He slumps in a chair.* SOPHIE *sits in another chair, opposite him.*)

88. EXT. VIENNA. NIGHT

Black-and-white newsreel images: 1937. Nazi supporters are marching in the streets in a huge torch-light parade. Searchlights play across the crowd, catching faces, insignia and faces of onlookers in windows in the streets behind the crowd. The blazing torches carried by the demonstrators hiss in an otherwise eerie silence.

89. INT. ALEXANDER'S APARTMENT. DAY

ALEXANDER *and* SOPHIE *are sitting in their chairs, lost in their separate preoccupations.* ALEXANDER *suddenly turns and looks at* SOPHIE.

ALEXANDER: Nina knew everything. She would never say anything. Just appear at the café at the end of the day and walk me home. I'd bring her éclairs. She loved éclairs. I told her about the people, the customers, the way they ate their cakes. (*Pause.*) You know what the Nazis called the Viennese? Cream cakes!

(*Again he pauses, watching* SOPHIE*'s reaction.*)

Then the Germans came. We listened to the broadcast. The Chancellor said, 'God save Austria.' We knew they'd be in the streets next day.

90. EXT. AUSTRIA. DAY

Black-and-white newsreel: 1938. Columns of German troops are moving through the Austrian countryside towards Vienna. They pass a provincial hotel. Crowds waving swastikas welcome them. A young German soldier, on a troop-carrier, reaches out to people who line the streets. He touches hands with a woman. A column of German troops goose-step; their shadows are long and dark in the winter sunlight.

91. INT. ALEXANDER'S APARTMENT. DAY

ALEXANDER *and* SOPHIE *in armchairs, facing each other.*

ALEXANDER: We went to bed. In there . . . (SOPHIE *looks round to see the screen that conceals the room from behind which* ALEXANDER *went to get his waiter's tail-coat.*)

We lay in bed, side by side. In there. I knew she was wide awake. I knew she wanted to talk . . . something she wanted to tell me. But I went to sleep. (*He pauses, and it seems as though his anger is going to mount again.*) Her brother always said the family was pure

Aryan. But who didn't say that in those days? (*Again he pauses.*) She must have been so frightened, lying in bed, in the dark, in there, waiting . . . and I slept . . .
(ALEXANDER *suddenly looks up at* SOPHIE *very sharply, gets up and goes over to her and takes her arm.* SOPHIE *is frightened; she suspects he is going to attack her again. She tenses, recoils in her chair. But* ALEXANDER, *surprisingly gently, takes her arm and urges her to stand. She relaxes and lets herself be led across the room towards the kitchen alcove.*)
Next morning I came in here.

92. INT. ALEXANDER'S KITCHEN. DAY

ALEXANDER *walks into the tiny kitchen where earlier he prepared the tea. Even though it is a tiny space, he still manages to avoid walking across the middle of its floor. He keeps himself to one side, pressing against the cupboard. An old gas stove is in the far corner, the oven door slightly ajar. Opposite the stove* ALEXANDER *leans forward and points to the floor.*

ALEXANDER: This is where she lay. Just here.
(*He gestures with both hands to indicate the shape of a body. Then he slumps further forward and lets out a kind of strangled howl.* SOPHIE, *who has followed him into the little kitchen, steps up to him and gently takes him by the shoulder. She pulls him upright. For a moment their two faces are only inches apart. His face is suddenly drained of feeling. He looks perplexed, confused. He gives* SOPHIE *a sharp look. His voice is strained, dislocated.*)
You can't do it with gas any more.

93. INT. ALEXANDER'S APARTMENT. DAY

ALEXANDER *appears at the kitchen door. He stops, very*

tense. Then he walks with surprising speed across the apartment to the marble-topped table at which they have spent so much time sitting and talking. He pauses at the table, pointing at it.

ALEXANDER: Four suicide notes. She left four of them . . . written months apart . . . here.

(*He taps the table top and then speaks ironically.*)

A year's work. And I was the last to know.

(SOPHIE *has now appeared at the kitchen door, following him. But* ALEXANDER *appears not to notice her and instead walks rapidly towards the screen across the bedroom.*)

But that's not the point!

(*He reaches the screen and, with great violence, hurls it away from the doorway. Behind the screen is a large bed, old clothes, cupboards, dust, cobwebs:* ALEXANDER*'s and* NINA*'s bedroom, more or less as it was the day she killed herself.* SOPHIE*, who has followed* ALEXANDER *across the apartment to see the room that has always been concealed behind the screen, is horrified by what is revealed.* ALEXANDER *looks haunted, deranged.*)

We were married for twenty years. In the same bed. Night after night. (*Wildly*) I never had any desire for her. Do you understand that? I had to make myself. I loved her.

(*He turns, and heads towards the mirror. With the bitterest irony:*)

The breakthrough to the woman. (*Suddenly shouting*) What woman? What breakthrough? Remember. Just remember. That's what he said! It doesn't make any difference!

(*By now* ALEXANDER *is staring at himself in the mirror. Suddenly he sweeps his hands along the shelf below the mirror, knocking everything on to the floor: photographs in heavy silver frames, little bowls, bric-à-brac. As these*

things crash on to the apartment floor, he reaches up and begins tearing down photographs, flailing wildly at the mirror and at everything around him. Eventually his distress and fury begin to ebb: he lowers his head, resting on the shelf, staring helplessly at the wreckage around his feet. SOPHIE *has remained immobilized by the doorway to the bedroom. She turns and looks again at the double bed, with a quilted, floral bedspread, a night table with medicines, in the glow of an old lamp, pink bedroom slippers peeking out from underneath the bed, a scatter rug, a make-up table crowded with dusty bottles, powder, perfume, a sturdy, practical hairbrush, old frocks on a rack. A nightdress and a dressing gown are laid out on the bed. A 1930s straw hat catches the light that filters in through a high bedroom window. She realizes that she is staring into a mausoleum. She walks slowly across to where* ALEXANDER *is leaning in despair by his torn photographs. She looks at him; she struggles to find some appropriate words. A silence.)*

SOPHIE: We need some fresh air.

94. EXT. POST-FIRST WORLD WAR VIENNA. DAY

Black-and-white images: the Prater Gardens funfair. The big ferris wheel turns above crowds who mingle around stalls below. A miniature train, its open carriages packed with waving Viennese. Carts are pulled up the rails of an old-fashioned roller-coaster.

95. EXT. PRATER GARDENS. DAY

YOUNG SOPHIE *appears in a cart at the top of the Prater Gardens water chute. She is waving with one hand and clutching a wide-brimmed straw hat to her head with her other hand. The cart hurtles down the steep slope and plunges through the water below.* YOUNG SOPHIE *screams. As the cart is slowed by the water, she starts laughing. At the bottom of the chute, watching her and also laughing, stands* ANNA. *She is radiant; she waves to* YOUNG SOPHIE *and blows her a kiss as she sails by.*

96. EXT. PRATER GARDENS. DAY

ALEXANDER *is at the Spükschloss, a shooting range. Every time a shot hits its mark, ghouls and monsters rise from boxes; skeletons appear in cupboards; the eyes drop out of a hideous face on the wall; a monstrous mechanical bird flaps its wings.* ALEXANDER *is trying to hit these grotesque targets, but with an absurd seriousness.* SOPHIE, *who watches him from one side of the Spükschloss, is roaring with laughter: at the ghouls, at* ALEXANDER, *or merely with relief at having left the apartment.* SOPHIE *is wearing the cape in which she first arrived in Vienna.* ALEXANDER *is wearing a heavy black overcoat and an astrakhan hat.*

97. EXT. PRATER GARDENS. DAY

ALEXANDER *and* SOPHIE *walk across a large, open area, behind which is a vast painted oriental backdrop: the exterior of a particularly exotic roller-coaster. They do not talk to each other but walk together with an ease and comfort that comes only when extremes of tension have been broken by activity or laughter. They walk through a Prater alleyway that leads out*

of the funfair itself, and into a park beyond. They reach an area of huge chestnut trees and a small pond. It is a beautiful spring afternoon. The raucous noise of the funfair and city fades into the distance. The two old people are now embraced by the park, spring, and the sounds of birds. Many other people, old and young, are strolling along the avenues or sitting on park benches.

SOPHIE: I used to meet Anna in this park. I would steal away from home and meet her here. My father thought I was learning English. Anna and I, we called our meetings my English lessons.

ALEXANDER: So where did it all end, this romantic story?

SOPHIE: My romantic story? It ended here.

98. EXT. PARK. DAY

YOUNG SOPHIE *and* ANNA *walk arm in arm. They are in the same park as the older* SOPHIE *and* ALEXANDER. *The same chestnut trees; the same benches. But the absence of city sounds and the 1918 costumes indicate the difference in era.*

YOUNG SOPHIE: I told them I was going to the library. They believe anything.

ANNA: I'm not sure I should approve of this.

(ANNA'*s tone suggests that she is coquettishly accepting a token expression of love. As she speaks, she catches the eye of a passing man and turns to see him go by – and so disengages her arm from* SOPHIE'*s. None the less, this is a moment of intimacy and great pleasure.*)

99. EXT. PARK. DAY

ALEXANDER *and* SOPHIE *are sitting on one of a line of park benches. Near them, an old woman sits reading a newspaper; beyond the old woman, a young couple, arm in arm. Further along the line, a group of men feed pigeons.*

SOPHIE: They wanted to marry me off. I would have married but still slipped out. I was still going to see her.

100. EXT. PARK. DAY

YOUNG SOPHIE *and* ANNA *are sitting on a park bench under a tree at the side of the pond.* YOUNG SOPHIE *stares imploringly at* ANNA: ANNA *is looking away.*

YOUNG SOPHIE: (*Pleading, desperate*) I love you. I *love* you! (*Pause.*) Will you never take me seriously?

(ANNA *does not look at* YOUNG SOPHIE: *her expression does not change. She is steeling herself to reject* YOUNG SOPHIE.)

101. EXT. PARK. DAY

SOPHIE *and* ALEXANDER *are sitting on their bench. With a sigh,* SOPHIE *gets up and walks away from* ALEXANDER, *who stays very still, half-listening to* SOPHIE.

SOPHIE: (*Loudly, as if to make sure* ALEXANDER *will hear her*) She said I was very romantic. (*Now softly, as if only to herself*) She said, 'The child is not yours.' (*She stops walking. She is struggling with herself, to find what happened in the park so many years ago, to discover or come to terms with what she now feels.*)

102. EXT. PARK. DAY
YOUNG SOPHIE *sits on the bench, staring at* ANNA, *who is beginning to get up.* ANNA *stands for a moment, turns and looks at her, smiles, shakes her head, walks away.* YOUNG SOPHIE *stares after her, immobilized, horrified.*

103. EXT. PARK. DAY
SOPHIE *and* ALEXANDER *walk side by side through the park. They are small figures among the trees, between the manicured flowerbeds. They do not speak. The city hums in the distance.*

104. EXT. PARK. DAY

YOUNG SOPHIE *is sitting alone on the bench beneath the trees. She is still staring, as if at the exact place where* ANNA *has just walked out of her life. Slowly, finger by finger, she begins to pull off her gloves. Then she leaps up from the bench and begins to run. She pushes her way through the bushes, past flowering trees, moving faster and faster. She arrives at a path, turns and heads towards the park gates leading on to the street. In the distance the city sounds get louder: a tram is approaching, clattering, and then the air is filled with the grind and screech of metal brakes on metal wheels.*

105. EXT. VIENNA. DAY

A tram is approaching along its rails. It looms at the camera,

fills the screen. The side of the tram, the cobbled street, the rails, a glimpse of trees by the roadside – all these fuse into a single blur. The sound of tram brakes echoes, then fades. Silence.

106. INT. FREUD'S ROOM. DAY

YOUNG SOPHIE *is lying back, her head among some pillows. She is wearing a white blouse: for a moment it is as if she were in a hospital bed rather than on* FREUD*'s couch.*

FREUD: Let me put something to you. Every suicide's way of dying represents a choice. You fell . . .

YOUNG SOPHIE: I tripped . . .

FREUD: You wanted to have a child.

YOUNG SOPHIE: Whose child?

FREUD: Your father's child . . . and Anna's. I know. Wishes are not limited to reality . . .

(YOUNG SOPHIE *grunts indignantly*.)

Anna would not let you share her child, so you wanted to die. You also wanted your father's love. So you survived your attempt.

YOUNG SOPHIE: How very ingenious.

FREUD: (*Suppressing anger*) It's as if I were taking you on a tour of a museum. Every time I try to explain one of the exhibits, you say, 'How very interesting. How ingenious.' As if it had nothing to do with you.

YOUNG SOPHIE: (*Looking up, and smiling sardonically at the invisible* FREUD) But I am in a museum. I'm one of the exhibits.

107. EXT. VIENNA. DAY

SOPHIE *and* ALEXANDER *are standing at a tram stop. A tram draws up in front of them.* SOPHIE *looks at* ALEXANDER*, at the wheels. He takes her arm. She smiles, amused at his gallantry. They board the tram. Almost all the seats are taken, but they find places to sit, side by side. The* *tram pulls away.* ALEXANDER *looks round at people sitting near him. He notices an elderly woman in a rather ridiculous yellow hat, and an old, very thin man.* SOPHIE *is interested only in the Vienna streets: she stares at the grand Imperial façades and at the little corner shops, their windows filled with cakes and sausage.* ALEXANDER *suddenly becomes aware of* SOPHIE*'s interest in the streets.*

ALEXANDER: You never wanted to come back?

SOPHIE: There was nothing to come back to. My mother, Uncle Aaron, my father even . . . One by one . . . all of them. Mauthausen, Dachau, wherever . . .

ALEXANDER: You could have . . .

SOPHIE: (*Decisively*) No. They thought they were Austrians.

(*She studies modern Vienna as the tram passes the Opera, the shops, the cafés. Her eyes search the faces of pedestrians: old women with shopping bags, young couples. The sounds of distant cheering become louder and louder* . . .)

108. EXT. VIENNA. DAY

Black-and-white newsreel: Hitler's motorcade arrives in central Vienna, the climactic moment of the 1938 Anschluss. Hitler is standing in his car, which rounds a corner of the Ringstrasse. Both sides of the road are packed with flag-waving Viennese welcoming him. In front of Hitler's car a small camera car travels. A cameraman, with a camera mounted on a high tripod, is recording this great event for posterity. The air is filled with roars of welcome.

109. INT. VIENNESE ARCADE. DAY

SOPHIE *and* ALEXANDER *are standing by a grandiose interior fountain. The sound of its splashing water echoes the fading roar of the Viennese crowd.* ALEXANDER *is staring up at the ceiling as if to show* SOPHIE *some architectural marvel. They walk from the fountain, down some shallow marble steps and along a magnificent corridor that leads to the glass frontage of a café.* ALEXANDER *stops at the doorway that leads into the café. He pushes open the door and, with an exaggerated, rather mannered gesture, invites* SOPHIE *to lead him in. She pauses, turns and looks at him.*

SOPHIE: So this is where you worked.

ALEXANDER: In my day it was . . . It was . . . (*He waves his hands to suggest the lost grandeur of the past.*) Now it's all tourists.

SOPHIE: Like me!

(ALEXANDER *laughs nervously, looks into the café, then suddenly seizes* SOPHIE *by the shoulders and pulls her back into the corridor, closing the café door behind them.*)

ALEXANDER: (*Panic in his voice*) Number 27! The woman who phoned. She's in there. How could she have known? How embarrassing!

(*Pause.* ALEXANDER *is utterly bewildered. Then he composes himself and begins to walk along the corridor.*)

I know where we can go.

(SOPHIE *eyes him quizzically and has to repress a smile.*)

SOPHIE: You and your women!

ALEXANDER: You and your Anna!

(*They walk along the corridor, past a grand marble façade by which they are now surrounded.*)

What happened to her?

SOPHIE: I never saw her again. I was packed off to relatives in America. Another kind of cure! Then marriage, divorce. Translating for a publishing house. Good novels. I translated Thomas Mann. And bad novels. Such trash I translated!

ALEXANDER: I should have gone to America.

SOPHIE: Perhaps I should have stayed. (*They have now reached the end of the corridor and begin to go down another flight of marble steps leading to doors that open on to the street.)*

ALEXANDER: What are you?

SOPHIE: You and I, we're people who never had children.

ALEXANDER: But your treatment . . .

SOPHIE: Why was I there? My father? Anna? Or because I disobeyed?

(They go out into the street.)

110. INT. FREUD'S ROOM. DAY

YOUNG SOPHIE *is sitting on the couch, angry, arms folded, listening impatiently.*

FREUD: *(With quiet insistence)* Sophie, you resist me because you think I have the power to force you to do what you do not want. But you have to cure yourself . . .

YOUNG SOPHIE: Cure! I don't want cures!

(Furious, she stands up, walks away from the couch and makes towards the door of the consulting room. She stops, turns and looks straight at FREUD.*)*

I want to be free. Of my father, of you, even of Anna. I don't want to be *cured*!

(She speaks through her fury. She struggles for control.)

I have *good reasons* to resist you . . .

FREUD: I'm not your father.

YOUNG SOPHIE: *(Staring at him)* Of course not. Why do you keep dragging me down?

(Long pause.)

FREUD: *(Quietly)* I know what you're thinking.

(As FREUD *continues speaking,* SOPHIE *gets up and starts pacing, rubbing her shoulders in the cold.)*

But I must warn you. Patients who break off their treatment exult in their victory, only to find themselves trapped by whatever brought them here in the first place.

(SOPHIE *reaches down and grabs her overcoat, which is lying on the couch. As she whirls it over her shoulders, it catches on the painting of* Oedipus and the Sphinx *hanging over the couch, knocking it askew.* SOPHIE *walks out of the room. A door slams.*)

111. INT. FREUD'S ROOM. DAY

YOUNG ALEXANDER *on the couch, muffled in his huge overcoat, staring at the ceiling.*

YOUNG ALEXANDER: Two little boys are playing in the mud. A man comes by and asks them, 'What are you making?' 'A church.' 'Where is the priest then?' One of the little boys says, 'We haven't enough shit for a priest.'

(*The sound of* FREUD*'s laughter. Pause.* ALEXANDER *begins to drift. He smiles; his teeth glint, rather surprisingly, in the sombre surroundings. The smile fades. He seems to be losing himself in some unhappy memory. He begins to speak, but his voice has become very, very distant, very faint. No doubt he is talking about his sister, but his words are inaudible. He is concentrating intently. His lips move soundlessly.*)

112. INT. VIENNA CAFÉ. DAY

A large café, impressive for its faded elegance. Newspapers mounted on wooden reading frames are piled on a table. A tiered stand of cakes and pastries dominates the centre of the place. A waiter hurries to and fro. The café is busy but not crowded. ALEXANDER *and* SOPHIE *are sitting at a table at the side of a large pillar, which allows them some privacy in this very public place.* ALEXANDER *is lighting a thin, Russian cigar. The table at which they sit is covered with empty glasses and the remains of some cakes. They have been here for quite a time.*

SOPHIE: I never went back.

ALEXANDER: So in the end?
SOPHIE: What end?
ALEXANDER: Your treatment.
SOPHIE: He said I should find a woman analyst.
ALEXANDER: In 1919! A remarkable man.
SOPHIE: Yes, but where?
ALEXANDER: In America . . .
SOPHIE: No, no, no . . . Too many!

(*Beyond* SOPHIE'*s and* ALEXANDER'*s table an area of the café is roped off, where some elderly men are holding a weekly stamp collectors' get-together. The men, poring over albums, pass specimens to one another.*

ALEXANDER *keeps looking round at these stamp collectors.* SOPHIE *speaks softly, calmly*:)

I keep wishing I could find . . . someone who could tell me whether I was right to leave . . . (*To herself*) I suppose that's why I came back to find you . . .

ALEXANDER: He did us no good.
SOPHIE: He did his best. I don't know which of us is more ridiculous, you sitting here for fifty years waiting for him to save you, or me coming back to find an answer . . .
ALEXANDER: I used to collect stamps. I would come here . . .
SOPHIE: (*Interrupting*) Don't you see? You lay there on that couch and told him a story about the Revolution, about Nina. It became a story about your father's bloodhounds and your sister. I told him a story about Anna. He turned it into a story about my father . . . Which story is true?
ALEXANDER: (*Ironically*) Truth.

(*He rolls the word around his mouth and raises a glass.*)

Let us drink to the truth.

(*He puts the glass down.*)

He was right . . . Yes, yes, I know what you're

thinking. I never changed. All my life the same . . .

SOPHIE: You could have been different . . .

ALEXANDER: (*Stubbornly*) I was not cured.

SOPHIE: Cured of what? A Revolution? Your life?

ALEXANDER: (*Quietly*) There must be answers . . .

(ALEXANDER *looks up and notices an old and tired woman at a counter over which she passes dirty dishes to dishwashers. She is wearing a drab uniform. Beyond her he sees the steam-filled kitchens at the back of the café. He looks back at* SOPHIE.)

I needed an answer. (*Pause.*) I remember once, I fell silent. I looked over my shoulder. (*Pause.*) He was bent over. He had his head in his hands. He was in complete despair. Was it something that I said?

SOPHIE: What would he make of us now?

ALEXANDER: He had his ideas too long ago. (SOPHIE *wants to reply and begins to gesture.* ALEXANDER *seizes her arm and stops her from speaking.*)

Life is very long. (*Suddenly spitting the words at her*) We didn't learn that in the treatment, did we?

(SOPHIE *stares at him.* ALEXANDER *is still gripping her arm.*)

Stay. You don't have to go back. We are the only ones left. We understand each other. I shall look after you.

(SOPHIE *looks at him sadly.*)

SOPHIE: And your two kinds of women? I don't want to be a sister . . .

(ALEXANDER *is mute, unable to react.*)

113. INT. ENTRANCE TO A VIENNESE APARTMENT. DUSK

At first a black-and-white still image: the hallway and stairs that lead to FREUD's *door. Then the banisters with their smooth wooden rail and wrought-iron supports.* SOPHIE's *hand is on the rail: she and* ALEXANDER *are walking up the stairs towards* FREUD*'s rooms.*

114. INT. FREUD MUSEUM. DUSK

SOPHIE *and* ALEXANDER *go in. They buy tickets. They go into the waiting room.* ALEXANDER *takes off his hat, hesitates, then walks into the consulting room.* SOPHIE *stands apart, somehow disengaged from the place. She follows* ALEXANDER, *joining him in front of the wall where the couch used to stand: now there is only a full-wall photo montage: pictures of what used to be there. These photos are sepia-toned and not very sharp.* ALEXANDER *peers at the image of the couch.*

SOPHIE: (*Surprised, a little amused*) Just photographs.

(*She approaches the spot where the couch was. Then a young couple, American tourists, pass in front of her, and her eyes follow them, wonderingly, ironically, taking in their jogging shoes, shoulder packs – and guide books.* ALEXANDER *has gone into* FREUD*'s study next door and is examining himself in the mirror hanging on the window catch: the mirror into which* FREUD *used to gaze when writing at his desk.* SOPHIE *comes up behind him, and he pulls himself up suddenly, a little embarrassed.* SOPHIE *walks back into the consulting room. She leans on the window sill, musing to herself.*)

It's so small . . .

(*She looks out at the trees in the yard. Her smile is wry but strong. She turns to* ALEXANDER. *He is bent over a cabinet, completely engrossed in what he is looking at:* FREUD*'s spectacles and pen in a glass case.* SOPHIE *watches* ALEXANDER *for a moment, then turns away with a gesture of irritation. There is nothing here for her to return to.*)

115. EXT. BERGGASSE. DUSK

SOPHIE *and* ALEXANDER *walk out of the entrance hall of*

the Freud Museum. The city noises are loud; cars roar past them. SOPHIE *looks up and down the street, sees a taxi, waves to it to stop and the taxi pulls up beside them. She opens the back door.* ALEXANDER *hardly moves. She turns to him, letting go of the door handle, and takes a step towards him. She takes hold of* ALEXANDER's *shoulders, gazes at him tenderly, and then kisses him. He swamps her in a huge embrace. Then she gently pulls free, turns and gets into the cab. It drives off. She does not look back.* ALEXANDER *is left, bewildered, anxious. He looks around him, unsure of what to do, what to think. Eventually he turns and walks quite fast, energetically, away up the street.*

116. INT. ALEXANDER'S APARTMENT. NIGHT

The room is in darkness. A light in the entrance hall goes on. The sound of the security chains. ALEXANDER *comes in. He switches on a light, goes over to the curtains of one of the windows and draws them shut. The broken and torn bric-à-brac and photographs are strewn over the floor. He walks past all this to the second window. He looks out on to the dark courtyard, then draws the curtain. He turns, notices the tea things on the marble-topped table. He stacks the glasses, lemon, etc., on a tray and carries it into the kitchen. He begins to do the washing up. He has forgotten to take off his overcoat.*

AFTERWORD

JOHN BERGER

Nineteen Nineteen speaks directly to what we know about life, composed inextricably of the most intimate movements of the heart, accident, and the remorseless movement of history.

All of us, whether clinically fixated or not, have been formed by experiences that still inhabit us. Memory is not only a trip but also a structure. Recollections are not only stories retold but also aspects of present feeling. Our hopes at any given moment are fashioned by our previous disappointments. Our need to share pain is as strong as our quest for pleasure. Every pain that is not purely physical is also retrospective. Our need to make sense of our lives has continually to take account of all this.

Of the creative media, the cinema is the most naturally adapted to deal with the folded past, carried within each of us like linen stacked in a cupboard. How often has consciousness been compared with a film, yet how seldom has the cinema properly exploited this aptitude. Millions of flashbacks have been used as mere mechanical explanations. 'Fade to memory' has simply meant 'Now you can see why'; or, alternatively, the cinema has been used to fill lakes of nostalgia in which everything dreamily undulates like water weed. In *Nineteen Nineteen* the stacked linen is unfolded with a terrible precision, layer by layer, and we see it laid out as the sheet of the present. Sophie and Alexander are lying on the beds that they and accident and history have made.

I have several times been told that the word 'ungainsayable' does not exist. I want to use it again. It is the quality that informs the cuts in this film, which moves, with a clarity that demands no effort on the spectator's part, between four layers of time, each of them omnipresent.

The first layer is that of the day an elderly man and woman spend together. The time of a bunch of anemones, of the moment when he takes a cigarette butt from between her fingers, as she weeps, so that it won't burn her, of his rage when he sweeps his collection of photographs and mementoes off a shelf, of their mounting gentleness and of the effort they are making to weep at the same time – something that they never achieve. The performances of Maria Schell and Paul Scofield are marvellously aligned: he is like an old waiter who has seen everything (it was the job by which he earned his living), she like a cat among cushions, deprived of a garden. In one sense both are prisoners; in another, they are partly freed because they can name their pain and be recognized by it. Neither of them thinks of courage; both display it.

The second layer is the time when Sophie was a young woman and Alexander a young man. (The two parts are played by Clare Higgins and Colin Firth.) We see each of them alone on the couch in Freud's consulting room, and we hear Freud's voice asking them questions and occasionally commenting on their answers. We also see them outside in the world, living their young lives: Sophie meets the woman she falls in love with; Alexander fences on one of his father's many estates. Neither of them can yet imagine being old; neither of them can see what is going to determine the future. We see the young person lying on the couch, speaking of his or her pain, and the film cuts to show us precisely the same pain on the old person's face, retelling the same story, reliving the same moment. Around the couch are cushions and a rug. The young person stares at the rug as if it was an incomprehensible labyrinth containing the secret of the future. Half a century later the old person recalls the pattern of the same unchanged rug and asks: why? Why did it happen like that? Yet in this second layer of time honey had the same taste as today and anemones the same colour.

The third layer is that of childhood. Alexander listens to his *baboushka* reading him Pushkin. It is a time of surface innocence, both emotionally and historically. Peasants harvest the grain on a Russian steppe. An indistinct figure, a gleaner, crouches on hands and knees in a field. 'They were the most exploited people on earth!' Sophie protests, as she gazes at the old Alexander with incredulity. And he replies, with a gasp that has in it all the credulity of childhood: 'They were our . . . our . . . We picked mushrooms together.'

The fourth layer of time is that of world history: the Bolshevik revolution and the storming of the Winter Palace. We see black-and-white newsreels showing, more eloquently than any thesis, the force of the masses demanding justice during the inevitable season of revolution that followed the countless winters of oppression and hunger. Alexander's sister, for whom he had a passion he dared not acknowledge, reneged on her family and joined the Red Army as a nurse. The *Anschluss* and the German Nazi entry into Vienna, the streets packed with welcoming crowds waving swastikas, the rounding up of Jews. Alexander's wife, unbeknown to him after nearly twenty years of living together, was Jewish. This fourth layer involves the hopes and sufferings of many millions, yet its scale cannot diminish by one iota what breaks in the heart of two individuals.

Life continues. The day of the bunch of anemones unfolds towards late afternoon. The pair of them leave the apartment and take a tram along the streets where so many Viennese, forty years before, hysterically welcomed Hitler, standing up in his limousine. They sit on a bench in the park where Sophie, when young, saw her beloved for the last time. They pass the tram stop where she threw herself on the lines to kill herself. But of none of this do they speak. They make their way to Freud's apartment, which is now a museum. In the museum there is a photograph of the couch, the cushions and the rug. Why? Why did it happen like that?

Nineteen Nineteen holds all these layers of time together, moving from one to another, holding them together as experience, yet *never leaving the present*.

We have come a long way. We started with a White Russian relic and a neurotic American woman. Many of us would believe that there were more urgent and more universal subjects to make a film about. Now, lucid but tear-stained, we know that we were wrong.

It is becoming more and more apparent, as our century nears its end, that the most valid testimonies to its history need to include the intimate, the almost sacredly private, and the gigantic historical currents that have rendered it indescribably cruel. If people speak of the end of ideology, it is because ideology, in its passion for the average and the typical, hates the private. And if it is clear that the bourgeois novel and bourgeois politics are moribund, it is because they cannot, by definition, see beyond the private circle.

The true stories of our time have to be able to reconcile a pile of clothes in a drawer with world historical upheavals. Such reconciliations pose many problems for the storyteller. The originality of *Nineteen Nineteen* as a film is that it offers an example of how this problem can be addressed and of how a story must speak to what we know in our hearts.